"十三五"国家重点图书
中国南方民间文学典籍英译丛书
丛书主编 张立玉 丛书副主编 起国庆

哭嫁歌

向金云 向秀云 讲唱 向代元 肖本正 搜集整理
蔡蔚 英译
石定乐 审校

WAILING SONGS AT WEDDING

出品单位：
中南民族大学南方少数民族文库翻译研究基地

武汉大学出版社

·汉英对照·

图书在版编目(CIP)数据

哭嫁歌=Wailing Songs at Wedding:汉英对照/向代元,肖本正搜集整理;蔡蔚英译.—武汉:武汉大学出版社,2021.7(2022.1重印)
中国南方民间文学典籍英译丛书/张立玉主编
"十三五"国家重点图书　2020年度国家出版基金资助项目
ISBN 978-7-307-22202-1

Ⅰ.哭… Ⅱ.①向… ②肖… ③蔡… Ⅲ.土家族—民间歌谣—作品集—中国—汉、英 Ⅳ.I277.291.3

中国版本图书馆 CIP 数据核字(2021)第 063285 号

责任编辑:李晶晶　　责任校对:汪欣怡　　版式设计:韩闻锦

出版发行:武汉大学出版社　(430072　武昌　珞珈山)
(电子邮箱:cbs22@whu.edu.cn　网址:www.wdp.whu.edu.cn)
印刷:湖北恒泰印务有限公司
开本:720×1000　1/16　印张:7.25　字数:87千字
版次:2021年7月第1版　2022年1月第2次印刷
ISBN 978-7-307-22202-1　定价:24.00元

版权所有,不得翻印;凡购我社的图书,如有质量问题,请与当地图书销售部门联系调换。

丛书编委会

学术顾问

王宏印　李正栓

主编

张立玉

副主编

起国庆

编委会成员（按姓氏笔画排列）

邓之宇	王向松	艾　芳	石定乐	龙江莉	刘　纯
陈兰芳	汤　茜	李克忠	杨　柳	杨筱奕	张立玉
张扬扬	张　瑛	和六花	依旺的	保俊萍	起国庆
陶开祥	鲁　钒	蔡　蔚	臧军娜		

序

近年来，民族典籍英译捷报频传，硕果累累。韩家全教授等人的壮族系列经典翻译陆续出版，王宏印教授等人的系列民族典籍英译研究著作已经问世，李正栓教授等人的藏族格言诗英译著作不断在国内外出版，王维波教授等人的东北民族典籍英译著作纷纷付梓，李昌银教授等人的"云南少数民族经典作品英译文库"于2018年年底出版，其他民族典籍英译作品也在接踵而至。

近日，中南民族大学张立玉教授传来佳音：他们要出版"十三五"国家重点图书——"中国南方民间文学典籍英译丛书"。虽叫民间文学，其实基本上都是民族典籍。这一系列包括十本书，它们是《黑暗传》《哭嫁歌》《哈尼阿培聪坡坡》《彝族民间故事》《南方民间创世神话选集》《十二奴局》《召树屯》《娥并与桑洛》《金笛》《梅葛》。其中，好几本是云南少数民族的。只有一本是汉族典籍，即《黑暗传》。很有意思的是，这些典籍展示了不同民族的创世史诗或诸如此类的东西。

《黑暗传》以民间歌谣唱本形象地描述了盘古开天辟地结束混沌黑暗，人类起源及社会发展的历程，融合了盘古、女娲、伏羲、炎帝神农氏、黄帝轩辕氏等众多英雄人物在洪荒时代艰难创世的一系列神话传说。它被称为汉族首部创世史诗。《哈尼阿培聪坡坡》是一部完整地记载哈尼族历史沿革的长篇史诗，堪称哈尼族的"史记"，长5000余行，以现实主义手法记叙了哈尼族祖先在各个历史时期的迁徙情况，并对其迁徙各地的原因、路线、途程，各个迁居地的社会生活、生产、风习、宗教，以及与毗邻民族的关系等，均作了详细而生动的辑录，因而该作品不仅具有文学价值，而且具有重大的历史学、社会学及宗教学价值。《南方民间创世神话选集》包括一些创世神话，主要是关于世界起源和人类起源的神话。《十二奴局》是一部在哈尼族广泛流传的民间诗歌，它通过"哈尼"（传统歌）的形式在民间演唱，世代流传。"奴局"是哈尼语，相当于汉族著述中的"篇"、"章"或汉族曲艺中的曲目。"十二奴局"即十二路歌的意思。译著表现了远古哈尼先民奇特的想象，涉及天体自然、人类发展、哈尼历史、历法计算、四时季令、农事活动等各个方面的知识，完整地反映了哈尼先民对天地形成、人类起源、民族迁徙的认识，具有创世神话与英雄史诗的合集之性质，可以说是哈尼族最为重要的文学经典之一。《梅葛》是彝族的一部长篇史诗，流传在云南省楚雄州的姚安、大姚等彝族地区。"梅葛"本为一种彝族歌调的名称，由于人们采用这种调子来唱彝族的创世史，因而创世史诗被称为"梅葛"。

其余几本书展示了一些少数民族的风俗习惯、恋爱故事、斗争故事等。《哭嫁歌》是土家族文化典籍。土家族姑娘在出嫁时用歌声诉说自己在封建买办婚姻制度下的不幸命运。《哭嫁歌》是土家族姑娘演唱的一种抒情歌谣，富有诗韵和乐感，融哀、怨、喜和乐为一体，以婉转的曲调向世人展示土家人独特的"哭"文化。《彝族民间故事》是一部以流传于云南楚雄彝族自治州彝族人民中间的民间故事为主体，同时覆盖全省包括小凉山等彝族地区的民间故事集。这些故事丰富多彩，从中能看到民族民间故事的各种形态和生动、奇妙而颇具彝族民族特色的文化特征。《召树屯》是傣族民间长篇叙事诗，叙述了傣族佛教世俗典籍《贝叶经·召树屯》中一个古老的传说故事。这部叙事诗一直为傣族人民所传唱，历久不衰。《娥并与桑洛》是一部优美生动的叙事诗，一个凄美的爱情悲剧。《金笛》是一部苗族长篇叙事诗，富于变幻性和传奇性，尽情铺叙扎董丕冉与蒙诗彩奏的悲欢离合，热情赞颂他们在与魔虎的激烈斗争中所表现出来的坚贞不屈、英勇顽强的精神，许多情节含有浓郁的民族特色。

这些故事都很引人入胜，都很符合国家文化发展需求，向世人讲述中国故事，传播中华文化，并且讲述的是民族故事，充分体现了党和国家对各民族的关怀。

民族典籍英译是传播中国文化、文学和文明的重要途径，是中华文化"走出去"的重要组成部分，是国家战略，是提高文化"软实力"的重要方式，在文化交流和文明建设中起着不可或缺的作用，对提升中国国际话语权和构建中国对外话语体系以及对建设世界文学都有积极意义。

中国民族典籍使世界文化更加丰富多彩、绚丽多姿。我国各民族典籍中折射出的文化多样性极大地丰富了世界多元、特色鲜明的文化。人们对多样性形成全新的认识角度和思维方式，有助于开阔视野，丰富思考问题的角度，挖掘这些经典中的教育价值和文化价值，对世界其他民族都有指导和借鉴意义，并且有助于建设我国的文化自信。

民族典籍翻译与研究事业关乎国家的稳定统一，关乎民族关系的和谐发展，关乎世界多元文化的实现。在中国，民族典籍资源极为丰富，有待进一步挖掘、翻译，仍有许多少数民族典籍亟待拯救，民族典籍翻译与研究工作任重而道远，民族典籍翻译事业大有可为。

李正栓[①]

2019 年 7 月 19 日

[①] 李正栓，中国英汉语比较研究会典籍英译专业委员会常务副会长兼秘书长；中国中医药研究促进会传统文化翻译与国际传播专业委员会常务主任委员。

前　言

土家族作为巴人的主体后裔，是一个历史悠久的民族，世居湘、鄂、渝、黔交界地带的武陵山区，人口835万（2010年）。土家族没有民族文字，富有特色的传统习俗承担着民族文化传承的功能，在传统民俗活动中，往往载歌载舞，很多歌谣因此口耳相传，世世代代流传下来。"哭嫁"就是一种独具特色的土家族传统婚俗，待嫁的新娘及其亲友在婚礼时边哭边唱，宣泄心中的真情实感，表达离别的不舍之情。这种抒情性的歌谣被誉为中国式的咏叹调，具有很高的艺术价值，2011年被列为国家非物质文化遗产。

这个英译本采用由向金云、向秀云演唱，肖本正、向代元整理的版本。全书共分10个章节，分别是哭爹娘、哭哥嫂、哭姊妹、哭兄弟、哭公婆、骂媒人、哭离娘席、哭梳头打扮、哭辞祖宗以及哭上轿。前5个章节是对家人哭诉，感谢家人的养育照顾，感叹彼此感情深厚，依依不舍现在生活，畏惧未知的婆家生活，家人纷纷劝慰，祝福未来生活越过越好；后5个章节分别在婚礼的不同仪式场景，如婚宴、梳头打扮、拜祖宗，以及上轿等演唱，传神地唱出了新娘对离开旧家的不舍，以及对即将出嫁的惶恐。

土家族新娘在《哭嫁歌》里唱出了人生命运关键转折时期的复杂情感，对父母的感恩依恋，对社会重男轻女的控诉埋怨，对媒人贪财好利的斥责诅咒，对兄弟姊妹间的友谊依依不舍，对婆家生活的悲观展望，并由此对自己角色转换提前做好最坏打算。据说，作为土家族女孩，在婚期到来之前，每当劳作之后，饭毕之时，亲友姊妹，聚首痛哭，边哭边唱。越是婚期临近，一家人的哭声就会愈加悲切凄凉。婚期到了的那一天，哭嫁便到了高潮。为了准备哭嫁，女孩稍懂事，就要学习哭嫁，观摩、学习如何哭，很小的时候就陪哭。陪哭的人，哭得越伤心、越动听、越感人越好。在出嫁前，姑娘如果不会哭嫁，会受到歧视和讥笑。在婚前哭嫁的时间短则五六天，长则一两个月。

"哭嫁歌"一直以来有多种译法，如 Wedding Lament, Bride's Weeping Song, Weeping Songs at Wedding, Kujia Song 等，都有一定的立场和理由。比如，Wedding Lament 这种译法强调了哭嫁歌的音乐性，突出了哀伤的旋律，且较为简洁直白，用作标题比较合适。湖北省人民政府网站的英文版在介绍土家族哭嫁习俗的英文文章中就采用了这个译法，从音乐角度讨论哭嫁歌的期刊论文也多用 lament 这个词，但 lament 这个词通常表达哀悼时的极度悲伤和痛惜，通常指挽歌，细究起来与哭嫁歌的内涵不太相符，因此还不太贴切。Bride's Weeping Song 的译法是从新娘的角度切入，比较有新意，但 weep 这个词强调心情哀伤，哭泣流泪，比较侧重默默流泪，不是哭诉，也没有高亢的拖腔之意，而且这部《哭嫁歌》中不仅仅有新娘的歌词，还有其他亲朋好友的歌词，因此也不太合适。而 Kujia Song 用音译的方法处理，作为标题太过简单，不能很好地达意。

译者选择了 Wailing Songs at Wedding 作为标题"哭嫁歌"的英译主要出于以下几个原因：首先，wail 这个动词表达的是高声哭号，通常用在抱怨和悲叹的语境中。此部《哭嫁歌》的很多内容正是体现了新娘在临嫁时对自己命运不公的诸多

前言

感慨，抱怨父母、哥嫂等娘家人急着把自己嫁人，悲叹嫁人后的生活再也不像在家做女儿时可以无忧无虑，而是要为别人家做牛做马，受人欺压，在内容上比较符合哭嫁歌的内涵；其次，wail 这个词有发出长而高的声音的涵义，而土家族的哭嫁歌唱起来声音较为高亢，又有很长的拖腔，因此 wail 一词也比较符合哭嫁歌的演唱形式。不仅如此，虽然有的新娘哭嫁会从婚礼前很早的时候开始，但其主要还是在婚礼前夜及当天的不同仪式场景中演唱，因此，译者认为，Wailing Songs at Wedding 能够确切地表达哭嫁歌的内容、形式以及演述场景，相比较起来更为适合。

《哭嫁歌》七字一句，韵律和谐，歌词对仗工整，较多排比，具有叙述性和抒情性的特点。较多使用文学中"比兴"的修辞手法，借景抒情、借物抒情，形成心情表达的一种境域。因此在翻译过程中，译者采用直译和意译相结合的方法，试图在英译句子中也使用结构一致的排比句，并着力捕捉字词间的微妙情感，力图将其叙述性、抒情性以及文学性完整体现。翻译过程中未免有疏漏不足之处，恳请读者指正，以便以后修订。

蔡蔚

2020 年 12 月

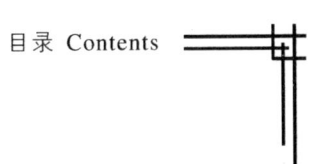

目　录

一、哭爹娘 …………………………………… 2
二、哭哥嫂 …………………………………… 28
三、哭姊妹 …………………………………… 42
四、哭兄弟 …………………………………… 56
五、哭公婆 …………………………………… 60
六、骂媒人 …………………………………… 64
七、哭离娘席 ………………………………… 72
八、哭梳头打扮 ……………………………… 80
九、哭辞祖宗 ………………………………… 92
十、哭上轿 …………………………………… 96

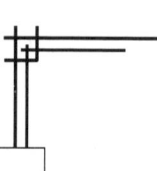

Contents

Chapter 1　To Mother and Father ·················· 3
Chapter 2　To Elder Brother and Sister-in-law ·········· 29
Chapter 3　To Sisters ························· 43
Chapter 4　To Younger Brothers ··················· 57
Chapter 5　To Grandparents ····················· 61
Chapter 6　Cursing the Matchmaker ················· 65
Chapter 7　On "Leaving-mom" Wedding Feast ··········· 73
Chapter 8　On Dressing and Glooming ··············· 81
Chapter 9　On Worshipping Ancestors ··············· 93
Chapter 10　On Entering into the Sedan ·············· 97

一、哭爹娘

女哭：
我的爹也，
我的娘呀！
安……吭吭①

铜盆打水透底清，
女儿今日离双亲。
安……吭吭

铜盆打水透底明，
从此女儿当贱人。
安……吭吭

父母养来父母生，
今日离娘放悲声。

---

① 安……吭吭，是哭嫁时表示悲声的衬词，一般哭两句加一句衬词。

一、哭爹娘 Chapter 1 To Mother and Father

Chapter 1 To Mother and Father

Bride's libretto:
Oh, my dear father!
Oh, my dear mother!
An—ang—ang①

The bottom of the copper pot can be seen clearly when it fetches water.
Today the one who is leaving you is your daughter.
An—ang—ang

The bottom of the copper pot can be seen brightly when it fetches water.
Today the one who will become lowly is your daughter.
An—ang—ang

I was given birth and raised up by you my parents,
It is hard to be away from you without crying today.

---

① An—ang—ang: It is padding syllables to imitate crying sounds and express sadness while singing this wailing song. They are usually used after two lines of lyrics.

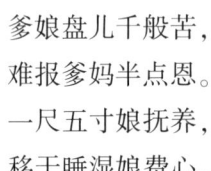

哭嫁歌 Wailing Songs at Wedding

爹娘盘儿千般苦，
难报爹妈半点恩。
一尺五寸娘抚养，
移干睡湿娘费心。

洗脸梳头娘辛苦，
长大侍奉别人亲。
我的爹呀我的娘。
咸腌萝卜淡操心，
我娘操的空头心，
我娘盘的空头人。
鸡母错抱鸭儿蛋，
画眉错投阳雀生。
盘成长大各自飞，
娘在东来儿在西。
堂屋打伞二重天，
亲生父母丢一边。
我的爹也，
我的娘呀！
安……吭吭

你的女儿从今后，
我要头顶别人的天。
我要脚踩别人地，
冤家脚踩是生地。

一、哭爹娘　Chapter 1　To Mother and Father

　　Hardship you have gone through in raising me up,
　　Nevertheless, nothing I have done in return.
　　Nursed, fed, as a baby, I was cared by mom every night,
　　Washed, groomed, in growing, I was helped by mom every morning.

　　Now, as a big girl, taken away by my husband,
　　I am expected to look after his family.
　　My dear father! My dear mother!
　　Alas... You have been toiling all these years for nothing.
　　My mom's caring for me has come to naught;
　　My mom's parenting has been in vain,
　　Just like a hen who has wrongly hatched out duckling eggs,
　　And a thrush who has wrongly fed a baby cuckoo,
　　While the growing duckling and cuckoo would flap away,
　　Just as what I am doing today.
　　My home stands in the east, but I'm marrying someone in the west.
　　My dear parents will be pushed aside.
　　My dear father!
　　My dear mother!
　　An—ang—ang

　　From today on,
　　I'll be at other's house.
　　Under their roof, on their floor.
　　I'll be regarded as a total stranger.

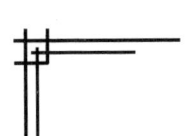

哭嫁歌 Wailing Songs at Wedding

人生要被别人欺，
马善要被别人骑。
十字街头杀独猪，
三沟两岔欺独人。
别人母子坐一排，
女儿一个当奴才。
服侍别人不到边，
冷眼冷语骂几天。

我的爹也，
我的娘呀！
娘边做女贵如金，
多亏爹娘养成人。
只想给娘做老女，
为何今日赶出门。
你的女儿不聪明，
怎么顺得人家心。
年轻见识少，
有力不会用。
有话不会说。

到了婆婆家，
婆婆门关紧，
脚板用钉钉。
父女几时才相见？
母女几时才相亲？

一、哭爹娘　Chapter 1　To Mother and Father

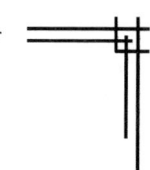

A stranger is likely to be bullied,

Just like a tamed horse is likely to be saddled.

Alone, a swine is doomed to be butchered in the crisscross street;

Alone, a person is doomed to be trodden on the sinuous mountain way.

As a family, my mother-in-law and my husband would be sitting together,

While I would be treated as a maid.

Blaming and scolding may last for days,

If I fail to serve them to their satisfaction.

My dearest father!

My dearest mother!

I am so precious a daughter staying with my mother

Thanks to my parents' upbringing,

I just want to be your daughter forever,

Why are you sending me away in such an eagerness?

I'm not smart enough,

How can I satisfy the in-laws?

Nor experienced enough as young am I.

With strength, not skilled yet,

With tongue, not glib yet.

Once I get into their home,

The door will be firmly latched

And I would be closely watched.

From now on, when can you see me, dear father?

When can you embrace me, dear mother?

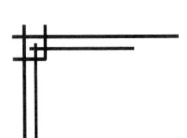

娘哭：
我的女也，
我的儿呀！
安……吭吭

你是娘的肉，
你是娘的宝。
安……吭吭

不是爹娘心肠硬，
不是把你赶出门。
树大要分丫，
女大要出嫁。
伏天一过阳雀去，
鸡崽长大离娘亲。
女儿如今长成人，
离爹离娘去成亲。

我的儿呀我的崽，
茅草难容虎藏身。
娘这阴沟的岩板，
不是你这龙行地。
人家的娘才是你的娘，
别人的家才是你的家。
要顺人家老的心，
要顺人家小的意。
你莫跟苦娘来加愁，

一、哭爹娘　Chapter 1　To Mother and Father

Mother's libretto:

My baby daughter,

My dear kid!

An—ang—ang

You are always my baby,

You are always my dearest.

An—ang—ang

Don't blame us as cold-hearted parents.

Don't blame us for pushing you for wedding.

It's well acknowledged that a grown-up girl is expected to be married,

Just as a grown-up tree to branch off.

The baby cuckoo would leave the nest after summer.

The grown chicken would not take shelter under hen's wings.

My baby daughter is a big girl now.

It's time for her to depart as to have a home of her own.

My dearest, my sweetie,

With a big girl,

My home is like a bush too short for a tiger to hide

And a sewer too cramped for a dragon to stay.

Your husband's mother is your mother.

Your husband's home is your home.

Try to be thoughtful for everyone, no matter old or young.

Try to be caring for everyone, no matter who he is.

Stop complaining that sounds agitating.

你莫跟苦娘来加气。
为佛要争一炉香,
为人要争一口气。

我的儿也,
我的崽呀!
你离了我这苦命娘,
脱了蓝衫换紫袍。

你离了我这苦命的娘,
拆了银桥搭金桥。
你脚踩葡萄丫,
你去当大家。
你脚踩葡萄叶,
你去创大业。
你脚踩葡萄藤,
你去当贵人。
你头戴冠花千斤重,
手提钥匙有半斤。
今天离爹离娘去,
发富齐天看娘来。

一、哭爹娘　Chapter 1　To Mother and Father

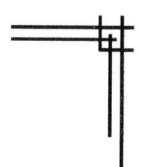

Stop whining that sounds over-hurting.

A worshipped joss still calls for more incense burned by pilgrims.

A worldly person, likewise, should strive for the better.

My dearest,

My sweetie,

Away from me—a poor mother,

You can put on purple gown to replace the blue one.①

Away from me—an unfortunate mother,

You can set up a golden bridge to replace the silvery one.

Stepping on the vine branch,

You will have the last word for a big and wealthy family.

Stepping on the vine leaves,

You will lead your family to a promising future.

Stepping on the vine stems,

You will be a lady respected and obeyed,

With heavy jewelry-decorated hairdressing on head,

And great bunch of keys in hand.

Bidding farewell, you are leaving us today.

Paying us a visit, you will be very fortunate someday.

---

① Purple gown is regarded as clothing of nobilities or officials, while the blue one is the commoner's costume.

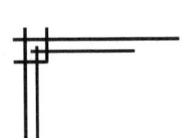

哭嫁歌
Wailing Songs at Wedding

女哭：
我的爹也，
我的娘呀！
安……吭吭

我娘怀我十个月，
十月怀胎受苦难。
十月一满临盆降，
我娘分身在一旁。
嘴巴吸得铁钉断，
双脚蹬得地皮穿。
醒来一看儿的身，
是女非男娘伤心。
女儿下地拳头大，
千辛万苦娘养成。
家中缺吃又缺穿，
五荒六月渡难关。
爹娘吃的对时饭，
喝的清水瓜菜汤。
口中节食养儿女，
没叫崽女饿一餐。

十冬腊月霜雪降，
北风呼呼刺骨寒。
你们穿的烂蓑衣，

一、哭爹娘   Chapter 1   To Mother and Father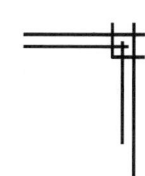

Bride's libretto:

Oh, my dear father!

Oh, my dear mother!

An—ang—ang

Carrying me, my mother suffered greatly for ten-month pregnancy.

The labor of delivery was even tougher and rougher

As the pain had been killing.

Enduring with the sharp and consistent pain,

My mother gritted her teeth,

While still pushing all out as she could.

Son in hope, daughter in fact,

My mother came out with disappointment at the first sight of me.

A tiny baby I had been,

My mother must have raised with painstaking.

Barely fed and clad,

The family suffered most during late spring and early summer.

Father and mother only had two meals a day,

Which was so thin as just a mixture of vegetable and water.

Parents did so to spare for the kids,

Who had never suffered starving.

In winter, it was frosting and snowing.

And wind was bone-chilling.

While my parents were ragged in clothing,

哭嫁歌 Wailing Songs at Wedding

女儿穿的一身棉。
你们挨了几多饿,
你们受了几多寒。

娘边坐了十八春,
刚刚学会做事情。
里里外外一把手,
一日三餐奉双亲。
如今女儿长大了,
偏生要离爹和娘。

我的爹也,
我的娘呀!
你们恩情比天高,
你们恩情比海深。
女儿今日离娘去,
成了世上不孝人。
倘若是个男子命,
奉养双亲到终身。
你儿是个小贱女,
长大侍奉别人亲。
天上大星对小星,
世上只有父母亲。
费心费力盘儿大,
不能报答养育恩。

一、哭爹娘 Chapter 1 To Mother and Father

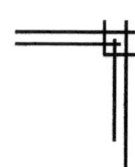

Just to get me dressed warmly.

Cold and hunger, you have suffered,

Year in, year out, you have endured.

Now I'm eighteen in the girlhood,

And have just learned some housework.

Capable of all the chores, taking care of my parents is my routine.

Three meals every day, without missing.

As your daughter, I have grown up now.

I have to depart and how hard it is for me.

Oh, my dear father!

My dear mother!

I owe what I am to your kindness which, if could be measured,

Is even higher than heaven, and even deeper than ocean.

I owe you so much,

But I can do nothing in return as I am leaving.

Could have I been your son,

You would be supported by me worry-free.

Nevertheless, I am just a little girl.

Born to be a daughter-in-law to take care of other's parents.

Big stars, in the sky, are shining on the small ones.

Parents, in the world, are the most affectionate towards their children.

No matter how much the latter could do,

It could be never enough to pay back the former.

哭嫁歌 Wailing Songs at Wedding

女儿是个菜籽命，
长大成人要分身。
丢下父母离家去，
叫儿怎么不伤心。

娘哭：
我的女儿也，
我的命心肝！
你的伤心流泪话，
句句哭痛娘的心。
女儿有情娘知晓，
哪愿骨肉来离分。
喜庆日子已选定，
吉时良辰要结亲。
舍不得来也要舍，
分不得来也要分。

我的儿呀我的崽，
你要千耐烦来万耐心。
到了人家父母前，
你要讲礼讲孝顺。
公公婆婆重重喊，
你嘛就要轻轻应。
你要体得人家意，
你要顺得人家心。
走路要看高和低，
过河要试水浅深。

一、哭爹娘　Chapter 1　To Mother and Father

As I am your daughter, it's fated that I am away to get married

Like a rape seed would fly away and land in other field.

Heartbroken I can't help getting,

As to you, farewell I'm bidding.

Mother's libretto:

My dear girl!

My sweetheart!

My heart is broken

At your sad tears and singing of the griefs.

I know you are reluctant to be away,

Neither you nor I am willing to be parting.

However, this day has been set since long ago.

Which is good time for the wedding reception.

I wouldn't let you go but I have to.

And you wouldn't leave but you have to.

My sweetie, my darling.

Do exercise your patience, as much as you can.

Because you should be polite and obedient

To your husband's parents.

Even addressed in a harsh tone,

Your response is expected to be gentle.

With understanding and empathy,

You'll get well along with your in-laws.

Mind your step, up or down, when walking.

Test the water, deep or shallow, when wading.

做事要看好和歹，
讲话要分老和青。
待人态度要和气，
兄弟姊妹要相亲。
冷茶冷饭你要吃，
冷言冷语你要忍。
勤劳苦做创家业，
起早睡晚身要勤。
东跑西跑莫乱跑，
是非场中莫乱行。
夫妻相爱要和顺，
要做敬夫女贤人。
婆媳相敬又相爱，
妯娌互助要互亲。
兄宽弟忍才和睦，
姐亲妹爱情义深。
团结才能有力量，
成事全靠人齐心。
一家同心合了意，
家发人发万事兴。
安身立命有途径，
我儿莫忘要记清。
事事照娘讲的做，
人家讲你有家训。
要为爹娘争口气，

一、哭爹娘　Chapter 1　To Mother and Father

Judge the behavior, proper or improper, when acting.

Knowing well the-spoken-to, young or old, when talking.

You can never be too kind

Particularly when dealing with your in-laws.

Take a leftover, no matter how cold.

Put up with the mocking words, no matter how cold.

Diligence leads to home fortune.

You should work hard day and night without pausing.

Don't get involved in any quarrel.

Don't put on a rubberneck for any dispute.

Could you be wise enough to respect each other,

You couple both can enjoy harmony and peace.

Caring and respectful, you and your mother-in-law are to each other.

With consideration and affection, you and your sisters-in-law treat one another.

For the family, understanding and gentleness strengthen the brotherhood.

While closeness and loving bond the sisterhood.

Solidarity produces power,

And concertation guarantees success.

One family of one mind,

The dream for property will come true indeed.

What has been said is truly right.

You should, as my daughter, keep this in mind.

If you follow the above instruction with no negligence,

You will be counted as well nurtured.

Live up to your dad and me,

要为哥嫂争名声。
只怪你娘无能力,
只怪你爹无志气。
该送三样无一样,
该送三种无一种。
怪只怪你爹娘穷,
想得到的做不到。
你勤扒苦做样样有,
你好吃懒做样样无。
如今你空脚空手去,
矮子上楼梯,
步步登高走。

女哭：
我的爹也,
我的娘呀!
安……吭吭

好儿不要爷田地,
好女不要嫁时衣。
难舍父母亲,
难报养育恩。

一、哭爹娘　Chapter 1　To Mother and Father

As well as honor the whole family with your good practice.
Alas, as your mom, I am incapable,
As your dad, he has no aspiration;
So we can't afford what you deserve.
It's a shame but we can't help.
Blame your parents as we are so poor
That we can't give you what we want to.
Nothing is unobtainable if one is diligent;
Everything is to go if one is slothful.
Now you are leaving accompanied by no dowry.
But your life will be better off,
As a dwarf also can go up by climbing ladder.

Bride's libretto:

Oh, my dear father!
My dear mother!
An—ang—ang

  An aspiring man would not be fed by the crops in father's field;

  An aspiring woman would not get clad with clothing made by her mother.

  Don't say you can't afford what I deserve,

  The fact is that I can never pay back what you've done in bringing me up.

哭嫁歌 Wailing Songs at Wedding

我的爹呀我的娘,
自从女儿出世来,
除了托肩无二层,
除了耳环无二银。
有穿有戴高处坐,
无穿无戴黑处立。
爹娘看我千斤重,
人家看我四两轻。
十字街头一把称,
一样豪绳几样认。
他只认他亲生子,
媳妇是他外头人。
人家老的不开口,
女儿有脚不敢走。
人家老的不做声,
女儿不敢向前行。
命苦不过女儿身,
从此成了下贱人。
落雨不得干处坐,
天晴没有树躲阴。
老的有理三扁担,
少的无理扁担伤,
身为下贱难做人。

一、哭爹娘　Chapter 1　To Mother and Father

My dearest father! My dearest mother!

Ever since I was born,

My only warming clothing is just the piece of shoulder padder.

My only jewelry are just the silver earrings.

The respectful seat is only for those who are well-dressed with jewelry.

While I am supposed to stand invisible as I am shabby and frumpy.

I am someone at home,

But no one at others.

A rope could be employed in different ways.

A person could be treated by different means.

For my parents-in-law, my husband is their own son with no doubt.

I, as their daughter-in-law, just an outsider.

Without my parents-in-law's instruction,

I have to stay still.

Without my parents-in-law's permission,

I have to get tied on the spot.

Once into their house, alas,

I would be ill-treated,

Not only exposed to the rain that is pouring,

But also to the sun that is burning

Young or old, reasonable or unreasonable,

Their people can bit me with carrying-poles.

Alas, life there is unbearable.

哭嫁歌 Wailing Songs at Wedding

我的爹也，
我的娘呀！
坐在娘家啥，
我脚踩莲花灯，
手拿绣花针，
太阳出来三丈高，
睡在床上未起身。
到了婆家啥，
我脚踩乱泥坑，
手拿黄连根。
太阳刚刚才露脸，
露水湿衣到半身。
十里山坡路难走，
五里茅岗难过人。
我越想越伤心，
我越想越害怕。

娘哭：
我的儿呀！
我的崽也！
安……吭吭

一、哭爹娘 Chapter 1 To Mother and Father

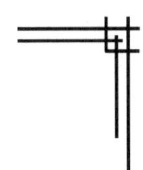

Oh, my dear father!

My dear mother!

At my own home, I have been so cherished

That you wish every step were on the lotus lamp when I am walking;

And everything were as light as embroidery needle when I am carrying.

I could stay in bed

Till midday if I wish.

While at their home, I will be so distained

that they won't care even I am trapped in mud

Or live a life as bitter as the root of coptis

I have to work in the field at dawn,

And get almost wet through with morning dew.

My life would be like the ten-li① ridge, which is said, to be too rough;

Or five-li hill, which is said, too tough.

The more I am thinking,

The more scared and sorrowful I am getting.

Mother's libretto:

My dear girl!

My sweetheart!

An—ang—ang

---

① Li: A traditional Chinese measure of distance, today standardized at 500 meters.

哭嫁歌 Wailing Songs at Wedding

你莫流泪,
你莫伤心,
你十分性子要改九分。
你出嫁出到好人家,
你从糠箩就跳米箩。
丢了苦的得甜的,
离了差的就好的。
离了穷的遇有的,
去了贱的得贵的。
你矮子上楼步步高,
你脱了蓝衫换紫袍。
伤心的话莫讲了,
伤心的泪莫流了。
我的儿呀我的崽,
娘的话要记心怀。
到了逢年过节时,
叫你妹妹接你来!

一、哭爹娘　Chapter 1　To Mother and Father

Don't cry.

Don't be sad.

And you are expected to be patient and mild.

You will jump out of the bran basket to the rice basket,

As your marriage is leading you to a good family,

The hard days and bad things will be left behind.

And the sweet days and good things will be forthcoming.

Poverty will be over,

And wealthy you would be.

Step by step, you are just like a short guy ascending the stairs to reach the high.

Finally, you will put on purple gown to replace the blue one.

Please don't say such saddening words any more.

Please don't cry which is breaking my heart more and more.

My child, my baby,

Bear my words in your mind.

I promise that I will send your sister

To pick you up at all festivals.

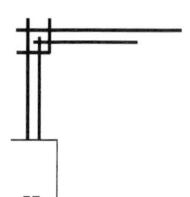

二、哭哥嫂

妹哭：
我的哥也，
我的嫂呀！
安……吭吭

哥哥堂中把壶提，
送你妹妹下贱去。
哥哥堂中把酒酌，
送你妹妹受挫磨。
妹贵日子今日满，
下贱日子从明天。
晓得下贱哪天止，
晓得下贱哪天完。
你的姊妹又不多，
今朝多了妹一个。
往日喊妹喊得甜，
妹挨哥哥十八年。
竹笋跟着竹子长，
哥哥疼妹十几年。

二、哭哥嫂　Chapter 2　To Elder Brother and Sister-in-law

Chapter 2　To Elder Brother and Sister-in-law

Bride's libretto:

Oh, my dear elder brother

And my dear sister-in-law!

An—ang—ang

My elder brother, you're carrying a wine jug in the hall,

As it is the day of my wedding;

You're serving the wine round and round

But you may not know that I'm about to suffer for my marriage.

My life is starting menial

As I am not a precious girl any more.

The menial life will be endless,

Though I hope I could see the finish.

You don't have many younger sisters in fact,

Why do you so rush to marry me off?

During the past eighteen years, we have been the closest siblings.

For you, I am always the sweetest baby sister.

For me, you are the bamboo, tall and strong,

And I am the bamboo shoot, growing up by your side.

哭嫁歌 Wailing Songs at Wedding

我的哥也,
我的嫂呀!
桤桤花开颜色好,
嫂妹分别在今朝。
你的妹妹见识少,
哥嫂恩高义也高。
妹和你们没坐够,
妹和你们没坐饱。
只想和哥嫂得久坐,
没想今日两分抛。
无娘鸡崽失了伴,
东跑西跑慌神了。
空中大雁失了群,
从此孤单我一人。
要想哥嫂再相见,
除非梦里得团圆。

嫂哭:
我的妹呀!
你莫寒心,
你莫流泪。
今天离了哥嫂去,
冷冷清清出了门。
难舍妹妹亲骨肉,
难舍妹妹一片情。
当年嫂到你家来,
你对嫂嫂好喜爱。

二、哭哥嫂　Chapter 2　To Elder Brother and Sister-in-law

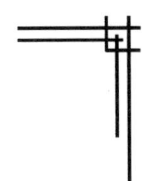

My dear elder brother,

My dear sister-in-law!

We are bidding farewell today

When the blossoms of gardenia are stunning.

I owe great gratitude to you, my brother and sister-in-law,

For your tolerance and caring for me—a girl little experienced.

It couldn't be better to stay with you.

It couldn't be enough to have your accompany.

I just want to be with you forever

And never expect to be separated.

I'm just like the chicken, without shelter of mother hen's wings,

Scared, flapping and running wildly.

I'm just like the wild goose, strayed from the flock,

Flying lonely and restlessly.

Rarely can I meet you, my brother and sister-in-law.

Only in my dreams could we get together again.

Sister-in-law's libretto:

My dear younger sister!

Don't get so desperate badly.

Don't cry so much.

Now you are leaving,

Lonely and grieved.

You are just like my own sister,

And I'm also suffering a lot.

I do remember when I just married your elder brother,

哭嫁歌 Wailing Songs at Wedding

姑嫂俩人好又好，
恰似骨肉亲同胞。
白日上山同薅草，
夜里同房把花挑。
妹妹心灵手又巧，
挑花绣朵样样好。
挑的鸳鸯来戏水，
挑的喜鹊把梅闹。
挑得好来绣得好，
鸳鸯喜鹊绣活了。
鸳鸯双双飞，
喜鹊喳喳叫。
同把喜事报，
喜事临门了。

我的妹呀！
聪明能干的妹呀！
后园石榴花开了，
你和哥嫂坐不老。
后园葡萄熟透了，
你和哥嫂坐不饱。
后园桃子离骨了，
妹妹离家在今朝。
今朝欢欢喜喜去，
三朝回门看哥嫂。

二、哭哥嫂　Chapter 2　To Elder Brother and Sister-in-law

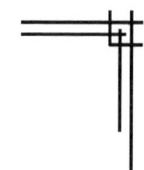

You were so friendly and empathy for me.
There has been a bond between us,
And we've had the sisterly love for each other.
Together, we mowed on the hill during the day.
Together, we embroidered round the table in the evening.
So bright and skilled you are,
That you are the best with thread and needles.
On your embroidery, mandarin ducks are playing in the water,
Magpies are frolicking on the plum tree.
With your outstanding skills,
You bring life to mandarin ducks and magpies:
Mandarin ducks are flying side by side.
Magpies are singing loudly.
They all make an announcement in joy
That something good and happy is coming.

Oh, my dear younger sister!
The sister so bright and competent!
The pomegranate flowers are in full bloom in back yard.
You cannot appreciate them with us now.
The grapes are quite ripe in back yard.
But you can't enjoy them with us now.
The peaches are to drop in back yard,
But you cannot pick them up with us now.
You should be leaving with joy
As we are meeting in three days when you are doing the returning.

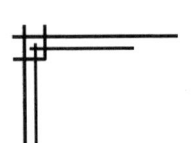

哭嫁歌　Wailing Songs at Wedding

妹哭：
我的哥,
我的嫂。
你们恩情好,
把妹当作宝。
妹妹做错事,
嫂嫂她承招。
爹和娘跟前,
常夸妹妹好。
嫂嫂要洗衣,
先叫妹妹斟。
哥嫂待妹妹,
耐烦又周到。
学做针线活,
嫂嫂常指导。
挑花又绣朵,
全跟嫂嫂学。

我的哥也,
我的嫂呀！
后园有根离娘树,
妹妹离娘有苦处。
后园有蓬离娘草,
妹妹离娘苦不了。
后园有座离娘岭,
妹妹离娘几伤心。

二、哭哥嫂　Chapter 2　To Elder Brother and Sister-in-law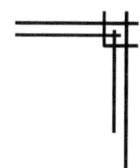

Bride's libretto:

My dear elder brother,

My dear sister-in-law,

You both have treated me as your dearest baby sister

For which I owe great deal to you.

Whenever I did wrong,

You, my sister-in-law, always bore the blame for my mistakes.

Whenever I did good,

You always praised me a lot in front of dad and mom.

When doing the laundry,

You always offered to get mine done together.

You both have treated me

With patience and thoughtfulness.

I would never forget how you, my sister-in-law,

Instructed me when I learned to do needlework.

You helped me with needle and thread

So that I could make good embroidery.

My dear elder brother!

My dear sister-in-law!

At the back yard, there is a tree called Leaving-mom Tree,

Which knows how painful I'm leaving my mom.

At the back yard, there is a clump of rushes called Leaving-mom Grass,

Which knows how heartbreaking I'm leaving my mom.

Beyond the backyard, there is a hill named Leaving-mom Hill,

Which knows how sorrowful I'm leaving my mom.

哭嫁歌　Wailing Songs at Wedding

后园有座离娘山，
妹妹离娘黑了天。
后园有座离娘坡，
妹妹离娘伤心多。
舍不得爹和娘，
舍不得嫂和哥。
舍不得爹娘年纪老，
舍不得哥嫂待妹好。

嫂哭：
我的妹呀！
我取方就圆的妹呀！
你少流泪呀！
你少寒心呀！
你往远处看，
你往好处想。
后园有棵离娘树，
离娘离爹人无数。
后园有蓬离娘草，
离娘人多跟娘少。
后园有条离娘岭，
离娘离爹多得很。
后园有座离娘山，
离娘离爹离得远。

二、哭哥嫂　Chapter 2　To Elder Brother and Sister-in-law

Beyond the backyard, there is a mountain named Leaving-mom Mountain,

Which knows how desperate I'm leaving my mom.

Over the backyard, there is a slope named Leaving-mom Slope,

Which knows how grieved I'm leaving my mom.

I hate to part from my father and mother,

Who have been aging and aging.

I am loath to part from you, my brother and sister-in-law

As you're the best in the world.

Sister-in-law's libretto:

My dear younger sister,

You are so admirable!

Don't cry so hard.

Don't get sad so much!

Think of the future,

And think of the positive side.

At the back yard, there is a tree called Leaving-mom Tree,

Which has witnessed countless brides parting from their parents.

At the back yard, there is a clump of rushes called Leaving-mom Grass,

Which can prove that most of them would have to leave mother rather than be with mother.

At the back yard, there is a hill called Leaving-mom Hill,

Which has witnessed a lot of girls moving out from their home.

At the back yard, there is a mountain called Leaving-mom Mountain,

Which can prove that most of them are far away from their parents.

哭嫁歌
Wailing Songs at Wedding

后园有座离娘坡，
离娘离爹离得多。
后园有根离娘藤，
离娘离爹大路行。
后园有朵离娘花，
离娘穷家到富家。
自古婚嫁天下同，
哪有女儿不离家。
南京养女嫁北京，
皇帝女子招驸马。
天上神仙也难免，
七姐下凡进董家。
劝妹不要太伤心，
收了眼泪莫哭嗒。

妹哭：
我的哥也，
我的嫂呀！
你们讲得对，
你们比得好。
人有高和矮，
哪有一般高。

二、哭哥嫂　Chapter 2　To Elder Brother and Sister-in-law

There is Leaving-mom Slope in the back yard,

Which can not tell the number of girls parting from their parents.

There is Leaving-mom Rattan in the back yard,

Along which you are going ahead after departing.

There is a Leaving-mom Flower in the back yard,

You will join in a wealthy family after leaving this poor one.

It is always the case that

Grown-up girls should be away from their original family for marriage.

A girl, brought up in the south, may have to marry someone in the north.

Even a princess has to leave the palace after the marriage;

Even a fairy has to leave the heaven if she gets married to a person on the earth,

Like the seventh female celestial descending to the world and getting married to Dong Yong.

Don't cry so hard.

Don't get sad so much!

Bride 's libretto:

My dear elder brother!

My dear sister-in-law!

What you said

Sounds reasonable and make sense indeed.

Nevertheless, how can I be a match to those

Who are the members of the royal, the wealthy or the heavenly?

哭嫁歌 Wailing Songs at Wedding

簸箕难比天，
妹难比神仙。
官家女出嫁，
还是她为官。
仙女来下凡，
还是她为王。
脚踩云梯步步升，
不是贱人是贵人。
你妹穷苦到人家，
冷冷清清难见人。
脚踩泥坑步步沉，
好比脚踩苦瓜藤。
好比江水去无回，
好比大雁失了群。
好比笼中鸟难飞，
好比家犬失主人，
千比万比比不上，
只怪生错女钗裙。

二、哭哥嫂　Chapter 2　To Elder Brother and Sister-in-law

As you know, their status are unreachable for me.
They are high above and I'm so humble on the earth.
A princess is still a princess
Even with her in-laws.
A fairy is still a fairy
Even with her in-laws.
For those nobles,
The marriage can carry them higher and higher,
While for people from poor family like me,
Marriage can drag me lower and lower.
With feet tangled by bitter vine,
I will be trapped in the mire, struggling but hopeless.
Married, I'm like the river, flowing away and never back.
Or, a goose, away from the flock, lonely with fear.
Or, a bird in the cage, that can't flee even with wings.
Or, a stray dog, that is so desperate and panic.
I hate myself to be born a girl,
Who doom to depart due to marriage.

三、哭姊妹

新娘哭：
我的姐！
我的妹！
一个柑子十二瓣，
姊妹今天要分散。
橙子好吃要剥皮，
姊妹相好要别离。
桃子开花满树红，
今天碰到刮大风。
只想姊妹永不分，
竹篮打水一场空。
月亮团圆团十五，
姊妹团圆哪一天？
梭罗开花十二台，
同父同母生下来，
姊妹各在天一方，
双亲大人丢一旁。
脚踩路边岩，
你来我没来。

三、哭姐妹 Chapter 3 To Sisters

Chapter 3   To Sisters

Bride's libretto:

My dear elder sister!

My dear younger sister!

We are just like the segments of the mandarin,

Used to be so close in bonding,

And today we have to be parting.

Intimacy among us turns out so painful at our departing

As the twelve segments are in separation.

We are just like the peaches blossom, red and gorgeous on the tree.

While departing is just like a gust of wind that makes us dropping and swept.

I have thought we could always stay together,

Alas, it is really a dream which never come true.

On every 15th day of the month, the moon can be full.

We are sisters in the family

Just like the flowers on the blooming Reevesia tree.

Growing up, getting married,

We have to bid goodbye to our parents one after another.

Over the path along the rocks,

You're coming but I'm not.

43

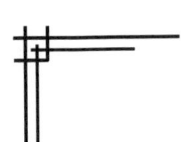

哭嫁歌 Wailing Songs at Wedding

脚踩路边草，
你来我去了，
同口水井没吃饱，
同个屋场没坐老。
姊妹情义深，
从小到如今。
同住一间房，
同睡一个枕。
吃饭共个碗，
洗脸共手巾。
春来同下田，
姊妹一条心。
跳舞又唱歌，
姊妹同个声。
挑花又绣朵，
姊妹一样新。
姊妹在一起，
从小没分身。
今日离姊妹，
哪有不伤心。

姊妹哭：
我的姐！
我的妹！
你莫流泪，
你莫伤心。

三、哭姐妹　Chapter 3　To Sisters

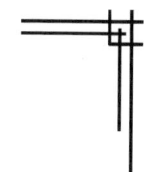

Over the path on the grass,

You're coming but I'm leaving.

We are never tired of living under the same roof.

We are never tired of drinking water fetched from the same well.

We are so sweet to each other,

From childhood to now.

We share the same room,

We share the same bed,

We can share everything

Even a bowl or a towel.

When working in the field,

We're side by side.

When dancing and singing,

We're hand in hand.

When doing cross-stitching and embroidering,

We're sitting around the table.

We never part with each other

As we're always together.

How can't my heart get broken

When we are due to be separating.

Sisters' libretto:

My dear elder sister!

My dear younger sister!

Don't shed tear.

Don't feel sad.

哭嫁歌
Wailing Songs at Wedding

离娘离爷处处离,
离姐离妹处处兴。
不是你一个,
不是你一人。
世上只有千年树,
哪有姊妹永一路。
世上只有千年鱼,
哪有姊妹不分离。
一个铜钱四个字,
娘家不能坐一世。
一个铜钱四个宝,
娘家好坐坐不老。
娘家不是虎坐的山,
娘家不是龙游的潭。
婆家才是久住处,
婆家才是创业地。

我的姐呀!
我的妹呀!
流泪眼观流泪眼,
断肠人送断肠人。
你我都是菜籽命,
搬到岩上要定根。
凉水好当不得酒,
娘家好坐不久留。

三、哭姐妹　Chapter 3　To Sisters

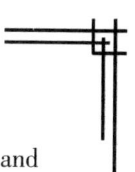

It's often the case one has to be parted from parents and sisters.

It's also well believed this parting leads to prosperity.

So you are not the only one

Who is suffering this parting.

A tree may stand for a millennium.

But how can sisters be never parting?

Fish has existed for a millennium.

But how can sisters be never parting?

There are four characters on the copper coin.

And a daughter cannot stay in the family for lifelong.

There are four blessings on the copper coin.

And a daughter can't count on parents' home for lifelong.

Parents' family is cozy but too small for the tiger.

Parents' family is comfortable but too shallow for the dragon.

Your husband's home is the proper place for you

To set and develop for your own.

My elder sister!

My younger sister!

We look at each other, all with tearful eyes.

We bit farewell, all with broken heart.

Just like the mustard seeds which can be rooted on the rocks.

We can survive wherever we go.

No matter how cool the water is, it can never be counted as wine.

No matter how comfortable the parents' home is, it can never be forever inhabitation.

哭嫁歌 Wailing Songs at Wedding

如果你我是男儿身，
房屋地基平半分。
田土家业都有份，
家先上面也有名。
这世你我命生就，
二世投胎转男生。

新娘哭：
我的姐呀！
我的妹呀！
你我都是苦命女，
都要离爹离娘去。
生错八字穿错衣，
找错庙门敬错神。
爹娘拖女挨了多少饿，
吃了多少亏。
苦了苦了为人家哭，
累了累了为人家累。
是个男儿身，
读书进学堂。
起屋上屋梁。
是个女儿命，
不得进学堂，
不得共屋场。

三、哭姐妹 Chapter 3 To Sisters

Just because we are not sons,

Who are entitled to heritage to the property of the family

—for us, no house, no field, no fortune, no money,

And no room on family tree.

It's no use to complain,

Just pray for the reincarnation that we could be sons.

Bride's libretto:

My dear elder sister!

My dear younger sister!

All of us are miserable,

As we are doomed to be away from our parents.

At wrong hour, in wrong date, in wrong clothes were we born,

To wrong temples, and wrong gods we kowtow,

That has led to the wrongs to everything.

Many a time, hardship, losing, starving,

Our parents have gone through to raise daughters like us.

However, at last, only pains, no gains,

As finally we have to marry to someone and get to other's home.

If we were sons,

We could go to school,

And we could set the main beam on the roof for house building.

But we are born to be daughters,

We are not allowed to go to school even we are smart,

And we are not expected to share the house with our brothers.

哭嫁歌 Wailing Songs at Wedding

读书没福分,
起屋坐不长。
不得敬家先,
不得侍爹娘。
是个男儿身,
讨亲接进门。

红红绿绿喜盈盈,
堂屋对子亮沉沉。
传宗接代不改姓,
家毫纸上也有名。
是个女儿命,
冷冷清清嫁出门。
去到他乡做贱人。
到了他乡受人欺,
爹娘不是自己的。
虽然跟他做儿媳,
鸡蛋隔了几层皮。
他一样茶饭几样办,
一样的儿女几样待。

三、哭姐妹 Chapter 3 To Sisters

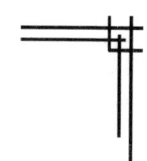

We have no luck to study in the school,

And we are not blessed so we cannot stay long in the new house.

We are unable to pay homage to our ancestors any longer,

Nor take care of our parents any longer, either.

If we were a son,

We could get a wife at home.

When the house was beautifully decorated for the wedding reception,

The red couplets in the central room bright up and lanterns light up.

The son can carry the family name as he can continue the ancestral line.

Therefore son's name is always kept on the family credence table.

On the contrary, when a daughter is married,

The house needs no decoration, no couplets, no lanterns.

As someone's wife, we are not counted at all.

We are then addressed as daughter-in-law,

Being just in-law, not with blood ties, we are doomed to be bullied.

Unlike our own parents, the in-laws would not treat me fairly.

Nor equally with their own sons and daughters.

We may have food similar in look, while the worst is always mine.

We may carry the pack basket similar in look,

一样的背笼几样装。
一样的功夫几样派。
一样的房门几样锁，
一样的朝门几样开。
明锁锁的他女儿，
暗锁锁的我外来人。

我的姐呀，
我的妹呀！
这样的日子我怎么过？
这样的爹娘我怎么坐？
做不得的要你做，
吃不得的要你吃。
做了人家的媳妇，
千斤担子要你挑。
端了人家的碗，
受了人家的管。
过了人家门，
成了人家人。
人家不开口，
有脚不敢走，
人家不安排，
有脚不敢来。

三、哭姐妹 Chapter 3 To Sisters

But with different load inside, and the heaviest is always mine.

The housework is assigned to all of us, but the toughest is always mine.

Different locks are on the doors.

Everyone has the keys except me.

They say they have to keep an eye on their daughters

But I know very well their doing so just on guard against me.

My dear elder sister!

My dear younger sister!

How can I put up with this!

How can I stay with the in-laws like that!

He made the same meal in different bowls,

Willing or unwilling, I have to do whatever I'm expected to.

Willing or unwilling, I have to take whatever I'm given.

As a daughter-in-law,

I have to stand being overloaded.

Just as the old saying,

The giver is the keeper.

Since I become their daughter-in-law,

They are my giver as well as the keeper.

Without their approval,

I dare not to be away.

Only do they plan for,

Can I pay my parents visit.

不得回娘家,
永世当奴才。
服侍老的一杯茶,
服侍少的不患着①。
人家老的放眼前,
自己老的放一边。
哪有不心寒,
哪有不心酸。

姊妹哭:
我的姐呀!
我的妹呀!
姊妹情义深,
今夜陪亲人。
情长夜又短,
别情诉不清。
姊妹收了泪,
切莫放悲声。

公鸡快叫了,
准备好动身。
月亮缺又圆,
自古到如今。
三朝回门来,
姊妹再谈心。

---

① 不患者:划不来的意思。

三、哭姐妹 Chapter 3 To Sisters

Since married, I'm to be tied to the in-law's,

Working as a maid forever.

I can serve the elderly a cup of tea,

But why should I serve the younger and the kids?

I take good care of parents-in-law,

While leaving my own parents alone at home,

How can I not get blue?

How can I not get sad?

Sisters' libretto:

My dear elder sister!

My dear younger sister!

So bonding as we are,

We stay with you on the eve of the wedding.

Even the whole night is too short for us to bid farewell.

As we have too much to say and too many to share.

Stop crying my sister,

And no more weeping.

The roosters are about to greet the rising sun,

And you should get ready for leaving.

Waning and full, full and waning,

Again and again, that is the way the moon is working.

It's for certain that you'll be back in the third day after the reception,

And it's for sure that we'll have a tête-à-tête since then.

四、哭兄弟

新娘哭：
我的弟呀！
天不平来地不平，
同父同母不同命。
兄弟是个男子汉，
你姐是个女衩群。
兄弟修得有缘分，
能和父母坐一生。
堂上父母要孝顺，
早晚侍奉要殷勤。
春莫饿来冬莫冷，
问寒问暖莫粗心。
若是忤逆不孝顺，
枉在人间背骂名。
高坡岭上天寒冷，
父母在堂莫远行。
若有三病两痛处，
赶快捡药把医请。

四、哭兄弟　Chapter 4　To Younger Brothers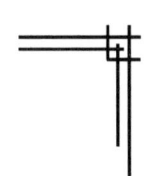

Chapter 4　To Younger Brothers

Bride's libretto:

My dear younger brother!

We are born to go in different ways,

Though we have same parents.

It seems unfair but I can do nothing,

Just because you are a son, I'm a daughter.

You are entitled to have the privilege of

Staying with our parents for lifelong.

Do keep this in mind: It's never too affable and filial to our parents,

Who should be well attended every day, year around.

You will be blamed even cursed

If you are not dutiful to our father and mother,

Of course I hope that would never come true.

Our home is sited on the top of the hill

Where is always chilly and windy,

Therefore you should not be far away from home

In case our parents fall ill and you are needed then.

If they don't feel well,

Get doctors and medicine home as quickly as you can.

哭嫁歌 Wailing Songs at Wedding

古人行孝多得很,
自古流传到如今。
孟宗哭竹冬笋生,
王祥为母卧寒冰。
董永卖身为葬父,
曹安杀子为家贫。
为人只要行孝顺,
行孝之人远传名。
你的姐姐生错命,
不能在家敬双亲。
我若是个男子命,
房屋田土平半分。
你姐偏是女儿命,
只能讲来不能行。
这些事情都靠你,
兄弟牢牢记在心。

四、哭兄弟　Chapter 4　To Younger Brothers

There are many stories to show filial piety in ancient times.

With his tears, Meng Zong watered the bamboo to shoot in winter.

With his body, Wang Xiang melted the ice on river to do fishing for his mother.

By selling himself into slavery, Dong Yong managed to get his father interred with the money.

To satisfy his mother with meat, Cao An had to kill his son as he couldn't afford to.

The above people's performance of filiality

Have been remarkable since the ancient times.

A man who can respect his parents will earn people's respect.

As a daughter, I have to get married away from home.

And I can't take care of parents as you do.

Were I your brother, I could take my share of the land, house, as well as the responsibility.

But the fact is I am your sister, all these is beyond practicing.

So my younger brother, you have to take all.

Do keep these words in mind!

五、哭公婆

新娘哭：
我的公公！
我的婆婆！
水有源来树有根，
万丈古树从根生。
公婆疼爱小孙女，
从小抚育到如今。
在家不离公婆身，
出门带孙去走亲。
孙是公婆随身宝，
公婆把孙当成金。
公婆恩情深似海，
孙女难报公婆恩。
只想婆孙得久坐，
哪知明日要离分。
孙女要离公婆去，
好比寒冬衣离身。
好比源头断了水，
好比树木断了根。

五、哭公婆 Chapter 5 To Grandparents

Chapter 5　To Grandparents

Bride's libretto:

My dear grandpa!

My dear grandma!

As there is always fountainhead for water,

There is root for a tree no matter how tall and how old.

You brought me up with love.

Where you go,

I'm always with you and your care.

You have been treating me as pearl

And counting me as treasure.

I owe you so much

And always dream to do in return.

But before I could do,

I have to leave for wedding.

Away from grandpa and granny,

For me, it's just like taking off warm clothes in chilly winter.

Or the water cut off from the source.

Or a tree uprooted.

哭嫁歌 Wailing Songs at Wedding

你的孙女生错命,
辜负公婆一片心。
不得堂前行孝敬,
不得侍奉到终身。
孙女是个男子命,
今日披红耀门庭。
孙女是个下贱女,
要离公婆要离门。
孙女不得行孝敬,
成了世上不孝人。

五、哭公婆 Chapter 5 To Grandparents

As a girl, your granddaughter is doomed
to be unable to offer anything in return,
For I will fail to look after you as I have dreamed,
Nor stay with you as I hoped.
If I were your grandson,
The wedding day would be glory to the family.
However, as a girl, your granddaughter has to stay humble,
Getting away from you as to marry the other one.
I blame myself for my poof performance in filiality,
As I couldn't do anything for you in reality.

六、骂媒人

新娘哭：
天上起了黑乌云，
媒人起了黑良心。
天上起云要下雨，
媒人起心坑害人。
高坡种荞不用灰，
人间结亲不用媒。
多个媒人多个嘴，
媒人口里出是非。
韭菜开花十二台，
背时媒人天天来，
娘不肯来爹不肯，
背时媒人打总成①。
媒人婆来媒人婆，
天天都来我家坐。
坐矮我家大门坎，
坐窄我家堂屋角。
带来灰尘几大挑，
踩平门前的山坡。

---

① 打总成：（方言）不断地劝说促成。

Chapter 6　Cursing the Matchmaker

Bride's libretto:

Your personality is as dark as clouds.

Dark clouds is the sign for the rain,

Likewise dark personality is the drive for evil deeds.

Without plant ash, buckwheat can grow very well.

Without matchmaker, people can get married very well.

Matchmaker is a trouble-maker.

Gossiping is the means of matchmaking.

As the leek that blooms endlessly,

The matchmaker drops day and day, tirelessly.

No matter how firmly my parents have declined,

You, the damned matchmaker, is always attempting and persuading.

Day in and day out, you matchmaker come to my home without invitation.

Our doorsill has been worn out because you sit on it hours a day.

Our main hall is cornered because you always sit in it hours a day.

Too frequent is your intrusion that has brought loads and loads of dust.

And flattened the hill in front of our house.

哭嫁歌 Wailing Songs at Wedding

河上有座铁板桥，
背时媒人踩断了。
你来求亲讲大话。
说了娘家说婆家，
你吃婆家一杯茶。
你讲他家顶正发，
你吃婆家一杯酒。
你讲他家宗宗有，
我想给你倒杯茶。
后园茶树没发芽，
我想给你装杆烟。
后园烟叶没断巅，
我想给你倒杯酒。
河里河水断了流，
豌豆开花荚对荚。
背时媒人想鞋袜，
想鞋子来做寿鞋。
想袜子来做灵牌，
板栗开花球对球。
背时媒人想猪头，
一个猪头十二斤。
媒人吃了死断根，
枫香叶子三角叉。
背时媒人想粑粑。
粑粑好吃糯米打，
媒人吃了死一家。
莲蓬开花水面浮，

六、骂媒人　Chapter 6　Cursing the Matchmaker

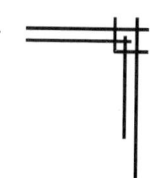

And trampled the bridge on the river—

A bridge paved with iron.

You came with a proposal as well as a lot of lies.

You lied to them about us and vice versa:

They served you tea,

Now you say they have a lot of money.

They served you wine,

Now you say they have things of all kinds.

I would serve you tea,

But the tea trees in the yard has not budded yet.

I would get your pipe loaded,

But the tobacco in the yard has not well processed yet.

I would offer you some wine,

But it can't be made as the river has dried out.

The blossoms of pea are in pairs,

She also wants to get the footwear from us, pairs after pairs.

Is she going to be in the shoes when lying in the casket?

Is she going to make tablet with the socks from us?

The blossoms of chestnut are in pairs,

Our matchmaker wants to have wine and meat.

She also wants to get the hog's head from us, which weighs twelve jin.

And it would stuff her to burst.

The forklike maple leaves are with three spikes,

And the damned matchmaker is greedy for baba buns

The baba buns is nice bite made of sticky rice.

But for her family, it would be deadly poisonous.

The lotus blooms on the water,

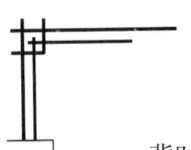

哭嫁歌　Wailing Songs at Wedding

背时媒人想酒肉。
想吃酒来抱尿罐，
想吃肉来舔屎板。
油菜开花一片黄，
背时媒人想衣裳。
青布蓝布各一段，
媒人穿起见阎王。
槐树开花吊线线，
背时媒人想挂面，
鸡蛋挂面黄桑桑，
媒人吃了烂肚肠。

紫木开花吊吊长，
背时媒人想银钱。
骗得银钱养老小，
一家老小都死完。
梨子开花一树白，
媒人全家死个绝。
先死媒人独生子，
后死媒人独孙儿。
媒人是个赶仗狗，
这头吃了那头走。
媒人手中有个瓢，
这头吃了那头舀。
牛栏背后栽丝瓜，
背时媒人生背花。

六、骂媒人　Chapter 6　Cursing the Matchmaker

The damned matchmaker wants wine and meat.
But for her, the wine will turn out to be pissy;
And the meat will turn out to be shitty.
The oilseed rape blooms brightly,
The damned matchmaker wants to get clothing from us.
There are clothes black and blue,
Both for the matchmaker to dress up in casket.
The pagoda trees blooms with strings,
The damned matchmaker wants to get noodles from us.
The noodle soup dressed with scrambles taste good,
But for the matchmaker, it will be hurting and make her sick.

Wisterias bloom in hanging.
The damned matchmaker is desperate for money.
The tricked money from us is to support her family,
But the whole family will all die on it.
The pear trees bloom as white as snow,
Nobody in matchmaker's family could survive because of her evil deed.
Her only son was the first on the dead list,
And the only grandson is after.
As a homeless dog, who is always hunting for food,
The matchmaker is always hunting for her interest.
She seems to be always equipped with a ladle,
To reach out for everything she counts profitable.
Back the cattle pen, towel gourd grow,
On the back of the damned matchmaker, the impetigo grow.

打扫堂屋让客坐,
牛栏里面关媒婆。
牛栏门杆紧紧锁,
莫让媒婆来打脱。

媒人哭：
天上无云不下雨,
地上无媒不成亲。
媒人吃了千家饭,
爹娘不肯我说亲。
青布裤子白裤腰,
爹娘嫁你你心焦。
不是我给你搭个桥,
你在娘家坐天牢。
你不要媒人不要中,
你背起包袱去找老公。

六、骂媒人　Chapter 6　Cursing the Matchmaker

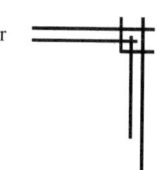

The main hall is cleaned for guests,
While the cattle pen is opened for matchmakers.
And then it will be locked tight,
So the matchmaker cannot flee.

The matchmaker's defense:
There will be no rain without clouds.
And people can't get married without matchmakers.
We have to go from family to family, and get declined again and again.
But we have to be committed to our job of matchmaking.
The black trousers is always with white waist,
The girl is always to be reluctant when urged to marriage.
Without my matchmaking, you might have to stay at your own home,
As in prison, lonely and pathetic.
Now you say you don't need a matchmaker,
Fine! Take luggage and start husband-hunting on your own.

七、哭离娘席

新娘哭：
天上乌云十八排，
十姊十妹坐拢来。
红漆桌子摆中间，
椅子板凳摆两边。
桌子高来椅子低，
十姊十妹请坐起。
上下的姐来左右的妹，
姐姐妹妹请安席。
楠木板凳三尺三，
有好客来无好安。
哥哥堂中把酒提，
你把贱妹送出去。
哥哥堂中把酒奠，
你送妹妹去下贱。
哥哥堂中把酒酌，
妹去他乡受折磨。

七、哭离娘席 Chapter 7 On "Leaving-mom" Wedding Feast

Chapter 7　On "Leaving-mom" Wedding Feast

Bride's libretto:

The black clouds are hanging over the sky.

My hanky pals are sitting by my side.

With the red lacquered table in the middle,

The chairs and benches are arranged on either side.

Tables and chairs are well set now.

Dear sisters, take your seat please!

All of my sisters,

Please help yourselves!

Three feet and a half in width is the wood bench,

And as a hostess, I can never be too entertaining.

My elder brother, you are carrying wine to one table after another,

And it is you that would take me off.

My elder brother, you are here making sacrifice with wine,

But from today on, I will be treated as a maid by that one's family.

My elder brother, you are here serving the wine to the guest,

But from today on, I will suffer a lot once away from home.

哥哥堂中把酒劝，
妹去他乡受落难。
楠木板凳五尺五，
有好客来无好主。

我今吃了离娘茶，
家也发来人也发。
家发如同水满坝，
人发如同笋子插。
今日吃了离娘烟，
荣华富贵都占全。
今日吃了离娘酒，
福禄寿喜样样有。
今日吃了离娘饭，
家发人兴有千万。

哭十二月花：
正月香花连二丫
满堂姊妹到我家。
二月桃花淡淡红，
今天姊妹都相逢。
三月油菜遍地黄，
我们姊妹要离娘。

七、哭离娘席　Chapter 7　On "Leaving-mom" Wedding Feast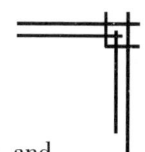

My elder brother, you are here making the toast again and again,

But from today on, I will be in trouble once away from home.

Five feet and a half in height is the wood bench.

And as a hostess, I can never be too hospitable.

As soon as I take the Leaving-mom Tea,

The fortune of the family will be booming.

The wealth of the family will be as much as river flowing over the bank.

And people in the family will be as many as bamboo shooting.

As soon as I take the Leaving-mom Tobacco,

The family will be flourishing and wealthy day by day.

As soon as I take the Leaving-mom Wine,

My family will enjoy longevity and blessing.

As soon as I take the Leaving-mom Meal,

My family will boom with people and fortune.

The Song of flowers year around:

In the first lunar month,

When we present fragrant flowers and burning incense to our ancestors,

All my sisters are arriving.

In the second lunar month,

When the peach trees blossom pinky and pretty,

All my sisters are gathering.

In the third lunar month,

When the field is carpeted with yellow rape flowers,

All our sisters are leaving home.

哭嫁歌 Wailing Songs at Wedding

四月梨花遍地开，
我是冤家和祸害。
五月兰花插起戴，
我们姊妹都相爱。
六月荷花朵朵团，
十姊十妹都团圆。
七月蓉花分七路，
你们都为我走路。
八月桂花一树香，
十个姊妹不一样。
九月菊花连九丫，
累我爹娘养冤家。
十月茶花落阴山，
我娘养我也心寒。

七、哭离娘席 Chapter 7 On "Leaving-mom" Wedding Feast

In the fourth lunar month,

When the pear trees blossom widely and whitely,

I should be blamed for all the misfortunes.

In the fifth lunar month,

When Orchid flowers are dressing hair,

All our sisters are sharing love.

In the sixth lunar month,

When Lotus flowers are shooting and growing,

All our sisters will be of reunion.

In the seventh lunar month,

When Hibiscus trees blossom are in glory,

All our sisters take a long walk for me and I owe you gratitude.

In the eighth lunar month,

When Osmanthus trees blossom are fragrant and sweet,

We may look different but we love each other.

In the ninth lunar month,

When Chrysanthemums blossom are prosperous,

My parents has been painstaking to bring me up for nothing.

In the tenth lunar month,

When Camellias blossom are all over the north side of the hill,

My mom is so heartbroken as well as in disappointment.

哭嫁歌 Wailing Songs at Wedding

冬月雪花遍山白,
我们姊妹要分别。
腊月梅花傲骨寒,
我们姊妹要分散。

红漆桌子黑漆椅,
满堂姊妹慢下席
无菜淡酒多添杯,
无菜淡饭姊妹吃。
十姊十妹都慢坐,
分别拆散我一个。
看到东方发了白,
姊妹留恋要离别。
看到东方发了亮,
姊妹留恋要分散。
姊妹人合意也合,
同得钥匙同得锁,
同得鞋子同得脚
姊妹同踩路边草,
离得多来合得少。
姊妹同踩路边岩,
你们来时我也来。

七、哭离娘席 Chapter 7 On "Leaving-mom" Wedding Feast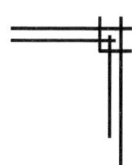

In the eleventh lunar month,

When the snow flakes shaped in flowers are painting the hill white,

All our sisters say goodbye to each other.

In the twelfth lunar month,

When Plum trees blossom are beautiful in chilly frost,

All our sisters have to part from each other.

Here, table red-lacquered and chair black-lacquered are well set,

And sisters, do take your seat.

The dishes might be plain and wine not good enough,

But still, I hope you try to help yourself and find enjoyment.

Ten younger sisters and ten elder sisters all sit down,

I'm the one to leave lonely after this gathering party.

When the sun starts rising,

That is the time I bid you farewell one by one.

When the sun is rising,

That is the time I'm setting out.

We are in such a strong sisterhood that among us there is no secret.

We use the same lock and we share the key.

We share the same shoes as we have the same-size feet.

Wherever one goes, the others would follow.

Whatever one has, the others could share.

八、哭梳头打扮

新娘哭：
我的伯娘我的娘，
手拿梳子心也寒。
你想人家红鸡蛋，
你想人家个个钱。
红鸡蛋来吃不饱，
个个钱来买油盐。
梳子虽小千斤重，
逼着女儿改面容。
伯娘今天狠心肠，
梳女头发要离娘。
梳了头发改了样，
从今以后当下贱。
往日梳的一条龙，
今日梳的重上重。
从前梳的一根辫，
今日梳的团团旋。
今朝头发往上梳，
那是梳的丫环头。

八、哭梳头打扮　Chapter 8　On Dressing and Glooming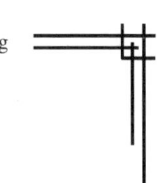

Chapter 8　On Dressing and Glooming

Bride's libretto:

My dear aunt, my dear mom,

You are grooming me with comb so hard and heart so cold.

You are expecting the red eggs from his family,

As well as money.

But the red eggs can't feed you full.

And money can buy no more than oil and salt.

The combs look tiny but weigh heavily.

You use them to redress me for wedding.

My aunty, how could you be so cruel,

As you are combing my hair for my departing.

My hair is newly dressed and my look is different,

So is my future.

I have been wearing my hair in a long plait,

But a bun instead today.

I have been twisting my hair into a braid,

But knots piling up today.

My hair is brushed backward,

And a life of maid I step forward.

哭嫁歌 Wailing Songs at Wedding

今朝头发往上抹
离了娘家去婆家。
今朝到了别人家,
受人欺来受人压。
生就的眉毛配就的相,
扯了眉毛改了样。①
一根丝线红又长,
扯我眉毛要离娘。
一根丝线短又短,
扯我眉毛要离乡。
一根丝线黑又黑,
生就的眉毛扯不得。
一根丝线青又青,
扯我眉毛好伤心。
一根丝线黄又黄,
扯我眉毛好可怜。
一根丝线透底白,
扯我眉毛好作孽。
扯了眉毛开了脸,
十人见了九人嫌。
我的伯娘我的娘,
你害了自己的女,
帮了别人的忙。

---

① 结婚的妇女要扯掉眉毛和脸上的汗毛,是一个仪式。

八、哭梳头打扮　Chapter 8　On Dressing and Glooming

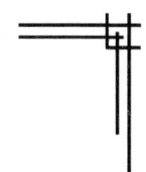

My hair is carefully pomaded,

And I have to leave for my husband's home I'm afraid.

Today I marry into his family,

Being ill-treated would be my destiny.

My look is like this, as it matches the eyebrow very well.

My look is likely to change as the eyebrow is trimmed.①

The silk thread, long and red, is employed to trim my eyebrow.

And I am, like the eyebrow, to leave my mom.

Now the silk thread, much shorter, is employed to trim my eyebrow.

And I am, like the eyebrow, to be away from my hometown.

Now the silk thread, as black as tar, is employed to trim my eyebrow.

And I am, like the eyebrow, reluctant to depart.

Now the green silk thread is employed to trim my eyebrow.

My heart hurt as my eyebrow is pulled out.

Now the yellow silk thread is employed to trim my eyebrow.

How pathetic I am to be removed from home.

Now the white silk thread is employed to trim my eyebrow.

How ill-fated I am to be separate from my family.

My eyebrow is trimmed and my face is hairless now.

But I don't like my new look, neither the others.

Nine of the ten who see me would get disgusting.

My dear aunt, my dear mom.

You have done something in favor of others, but against me.

---

① It is a ritual that a bride has to get her eyebrows and facial hair pulled out on the wedding day.

83

哭嫁歌 Wailing Songs at Wedding

伯娘哭：
我的女儿要耐烦，
不是伯娘狠心肠。
皇帝女子招驸马，
天上仙女也下凡。
昔日天上七仙女，
下凡配了董永郎。
何况凡间婚姻事，
自古到今世代传。
山中雀鸟要离山，
女儿长大要离娘。
脚踩楼梯步步上，
手攀楼梯上天堂。

梳了头发变了样，
穿了紫袍换蓝衫。
扯了眉毛改了样，
从今开始把业创。
拨开浮萍见清水，
拨开乌云见青天。
离了穷乡到富乡，
富乡得遇好爹娘。

八、哭梳头打扮　Chapter 8　On Dressing and Glooming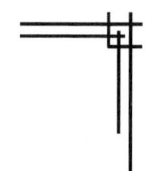

Aunt's libretto:

Don't complain so headily, my dear niece.

I'm not a hard-hearted aunty as you estimate.

Even a princess has to marry to a man.

Even a fairy in the heaven would search for husband by descending.

It's often the case the lord in the heaven

Marries his daughter to a nice man in the world.

Not mention for the ordinary people.

Marriage is something that has to be committed since thousands of years ago.

A bird is doomed to be away from the nest in the mountain.

Likewise a girl is bound to leave her mother for marriage.

For today on, you are living a life upgrading

As you are stepping up for bright future.

Not only your hair is in the different look,

You're dressed, not blue blouse any longer, in purple gown.

With your eyebrow trimmed, you are wearing a new look.

Your own family will be set up with good luck.

The water will appear clean only when the duckweed is brushed away.

The sky will look blue only when the dark cloud disperses.

You could get to the wealthy town only after you leave this poor one.

You would get great in-laws only when you go to a wealthy town.

哭嫁歌 Wailing Songs at Wedding

把你当龙手中捧，
把你当宝口中衔。
丢了银筷换金筷，
丢了银碗换金盘。
十人见了九人羡，
谁不夸奖美新娘。

哭穿露水衣：
我今天不穿露水衣，
不受人家老少欺。
丫环衣服我不穿，
丫环奴才我不当。
丫环衣服穿不热，
丫环奴才当不得。
今早穿了丫环衣，
成了人家丫环人。

哭穿露水鞋：
丫环鞋子我不穿，
穿了就把奴才当。
丫环鞋子穿不得，
离了爹娘又离爷。
今早穿了丫环鞋，
成了人家贱奴才。

八、哭梳头打扮　Chapter 8　On Dressing and Glooming

The in-laws would cherish you as dear as a pearl

And they are going to take such a good care of you with no neglect.

At your present home, your chopsticks are silvery,

While at the in-laws', they are golden.

At your present home, your bowl are silvery,

While at the in-laws', they are golden.

Nine of the ten who see you would get admiring.

You are such a pretty bride that makes everyone envy so much.

On putting on the Dress of Dew:

I really don't want to put on the Dress of Dew.

As I hate to be bullied by his family.

For me, this is the dress not for bride but for maid.

If I put it on, I will be their maid.

But I don't want to be their maid at all.

In this dress I will never feel warm,

I cannot be a maid or a slave.

Not matter whatever I think, this dress is on me now.

Alas, I turn out to be their maid.

On putting on the Shoes of Dew:

I really don't want to put on the Shoes of Dew,

As I hate to be a slave of in his family.

As soon as I put on these shoes,

I have to go away from my parents and my family.

No matter whatever I think, the shoes are on me now.

Alas, I turn out to be their maid.

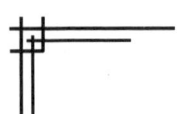

哭嫁歌 Wailing Songs at Wedding

哭穿露水帕：
今早搭了露水帕，
生离死别离了家。
今早搭了露水帕，
要受人家老少骂。

新娘哭：
我的妈呀我的娘，
你儿包了人家帕，
从今要听人家话。
你儿穿了人家衣，
从今要受他人欺。
你儿穿了人家裤，
从今要给人家做。
你儿穿了人家鞋，
从今一辈子转锅台。
你儿穿了人家袜，
从今难以回娘家。
这件苦衣我不穿，
身穿苦衣苦万年。

八、哭梳头打扮　Chapter 8　On Dressing and Glooming

On putting on the Head-chief of dew:

Now I'm putting on the Head-chief of Dew,

I will be separated with my family no matter how unwilling I am.

Now I'm putting on the Head-chief of Dew,

I would be ill-treated by his family no matter how nicely I am acting.

Bride's libretto:

My dear mother, my dear mother!

Once I have put on the head-chief from his home,

I'll have to be in obedience to his family.

Once I have put on the dress from his home,

I will be a push-over for his family.

Once I have put on the pants from his home,

My life will be of hardship and toil in his family.

Once I have put on the shoes from his home,

My rest life will be tied up in the kitchen.

Once I have put on the socks from his home,

I can hardly come back to my own home from now on.

I hate this outfit

As this means my suffering in the future.

89

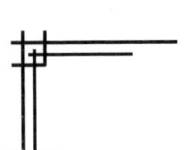

哭嫁歌 Wailing Songs at Wedding

苦衣裹身窄又短,
你儿穿起心里烦。
这件苦衣难得脱,
女儿一辈子受折磨。

八、哭梳头打扮　Chapter 8　On Dressing and Glooming

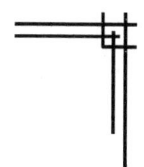

This outfit is so tight and short.
That makes me feel terribly lousy.
I'm afraid once it is put on it's impossible to take off.
I would be in endless suffering in the rest of my life.

九、哭辞祖宗

新娘哭：
我右脚跨出了娘的房，
左脚踩到了祖宗堂。
堂屋四四方，
红漆桌子摆中央。
象牙椅子摆八个，
乌木筷子摆八双。
全家老小一齐坐，
今天分开我一个。
今天是娘家的贵女，
明天成了婆家的贱人。
头发往上梳，
爹娘往后丢。
头发往后抹，
爹娘丢开啦。
我的祖公，
我的祖婆！
我脚踩堂屋中，
离了祖婆和祖公。

九、哭辞祖宗　Chapter 9　On Worshipping Ancestors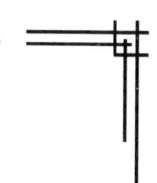

Chapter 9　On Worshipping Ancestors

Bride's libretto:

My right foot stepped out of my mother's room.

My left foot stepped into the hall where the ancestors are enshrined.

The hall is squarely shaped

With the red lacquered table in the center,

Round which eight ivory chairs are settled,

And on which eight pairs of ebony chopsticks are placed.

The whole family are sitting here.

Alas, there will not be a seat for me on my leaving.

As a daughter I'm precious with my people here,

But as a daughter-in-law, I'm nobody with in-laws.

As my hair has been combed upwards,

I'm aware that my parents will be behind soon.

As my hair will be combed backwards.

I'm aware that away from my parents I'm turning.

My great-grandfather,

My great-grandmother!

Now I'm in the hall

To bid a farewell to you both.

93

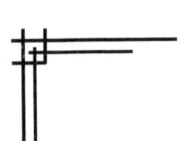

哭嫁歌　Wailing Songs at Wedding

我脚踩金斗四角方，
又离祖宗又离乡。
我脚踩金斗四角沿，
又离祖宗又离娘。

我的祖公，
我的祖婆！
这个头我不磕，
我不是你的子孙伙！
这个揖我不作，
我不是你们的香炉脚。
脚踩金斗四角方，
我手拿金筷十六双。
前头八双跟我去，
后头八双给兄弟。
前头八双跟我去，
我置穿来又置吃。
后头八双给兄弟，
要多买些田和地。

我的哥哥，
我的兄弟！
我脚踩半边月，
娘田爷地我受不得；
娘田爷地你们受，
父母在世莫远游。
孝顺父母你有名，
不孝父母枉为人。

九、哭辞祖宗 Chapter 9 On Worshipping Ancestors

I stepped on the four corners of the gold bucket,
As I am leaving my ancestor and my hometown.
I stepped on the four edges of the gold bucket,
As I am leaving my ancestors and my dear mother.

My dear great-grandfather,
My dear great-grandmother!
I don't want to kowtow to your memorial tablets,
As I'm not counted as your descendant.
I don't want to bow to your memorial tablets,
As I can't be the person who can hold the censer at your enshrine.
I stepped on the four corners of the gold bucket,
With gold chopsticks numbered in sixteen pairs.
I take the first eight pairs as my dowry,
And leave the left eight ones to my brothers.
With the first eight pairs of gold chopsticks,
I could purchase whatever I like —clothes and food.
With the other eight pairs of gold chopsticks,
You should buy more fields and real estates.

My elder brother,
My younger brother!
I'm not under the same roof with you any longer,
So I am not in the list of heirs for our parents properties,
Since you are the authentic heirs,
You should stay with our parents and have them in good care.
You will be praised due to your filial piety,
Otherwise you will be cursed as evil.

十、哭上轿

新娘哭：
看到东方发了白，
众家姊妹要离别。
看了东方开了口，
哭哭啼啼要抬走。
福好命好团圆坐，
福丑命薄我一个。
我脚踩房门角，
离了我的爹娘伙。
我脚踩火坑角，
离了我的哥嫂伙。
我脚踩堂屋角，
离了我的叔伯伙。
我脚踩阶檐脚，
离了我的团圆姊妹伙。
一块院坝四角团，
哥哥兄弟跟轿站。
灯笼火把两边分，
两壶美酒跟轿淋。

十、哭上轿　Chapter 10　On Entering into the Sedan

Chapter 10　On Entering into the Sedan

Bride's libretto:

The sun is rising in the east

When we sisters are bound to bid farewell.

The dawn is breaking in the east

When I am about to be carried away in tears.

You can stay together as you are blessed by good luck,

While I am the only one who suffers bad luck as a left-out.

Stepping on the doorsill of my room,

I'm leaving my dear parents;

On the fire pit,

I'm leaving my dear brothers and sisters-in-law;

On the threshold of the hall,

I'm leaving my uncles;

On the steps of the front door,

I'm leaving my dear sisters.

Like a courtyard has four corners, my sedan also has four

By which my dear brothers stand on guard respectively.

With torches and lanterns on each side,

The sedan was followed by the sprinkles from two pots of wine.

哭嫁歌 Wailing Songs at Wedding

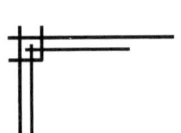

红伞左边打三转，
打在女儿轿跟前。
红伞右边打三转，
打在女儿嫁妆边。
大门面前三步坎，
深闺日子今日满。
大门外头三步梯，
离爹离娘离家去。
我的爹呀，
我的娘呀！
八仙轿子调了头，
一股财气进了屋。
八仙轿子打了转，
金库银库都装满。
财也发来人也旺，
年年四季享平安。

十、哭上轿 Chapter 10 On Entering into the Sedan

In front of the sedan,

The red umbrella is turned leftward three times.

By the side of my dowry,

The red umbrella is turned rightward three times.

There are three steps in front of the gate.

By crossing them I'm no longer a happy girl with my family.

There are three steps outside the gate,

On which I start my way from my dear parents and my sweet home.

My dear dad!

My dear mom!

The sedan turns around before starting off,

To make wealth go back to my home.

The sedan turns around before starting off,

To make wealth fulfill my home.

Blessed is my family with great fortune.

Blessed is my family with flourishing population.